It's a Blizzard!

Michele Coffey

Rosen REAL READERS

Rosen Classroom Books and Materials
New York

Published in 2002 by The Rosen Publishing Group, Inc.
29 East 21st Street, New York, NY 10010

Book Design: Ron A. Churley

ISBN: 0-8239-8224-6
6-pack ISBN: 0-8239-8627-6

Manufactured in the United States of America

Contents

4

So Much Snow

A blizzard is a powerful **snowstorm** with strong winds. Blizzard winds can blow thirty-five miles per hour or faster! The blowing snow makes it hard for people to see. When you can't see because of blowing snow, it is called a **whiteout**. During a blizzard, strong winds blow snow into deep **drifts**.

Blizzards can last for a few hours or a few days.

←————————————————————

Where Do Blizzards Strike?

In the United States, most blizzards happen in the northern states and the Great Plains states. The weather is colder in these areas.

Whiteouts make it **dangerous** to drive cars. Large cities can seem almost empty when a blizzard strikes.

Blizzards can make it very hard for people to even walk outside.

7

How Snow Forms

Before a blizzard begins, snow has to form. Snow forms when **water vapor** in the air gets very cold and **freezes** into tiny pieces of ice. Each piece of ice has six sides. The pieces of ice stick together and form snowflakes. When very cold winds mix with snow, a blizzard begins.

No two snowflakes are the same.
Each snowflake has its own special shape.

How Blizzards Start

Blizzards start when cold air moves over warmer land and makes warmer, wetter air rise. The place where the cold air and the warmer air meet is called a **cold front**. The cold front causes snow and strong winds, and a blizzard can start.

Many blizzards happen after periods of warmer winter weather.

Blizzard Dangers

When cold weather and strong winds mix, the air feels colder than it really is. This is called **windchill**. When the windchill is very low, you could get **frostbite** from being outside for too long. Very cold weather and windchills can harm your skin if you're not wearing warm clothing.

If it is 10 degrees outside and the wind is blowing at 10 miles per hour, it feels like it is 9 degrees below zero!

Blizzard Safety

If a blizzard is coming, make sure you have plenty of food and water at your house. Once a blizzard starts, you may not be able to leave your house for many days. If you  go outside, be sure to wear very warm clothing. Blizzards can be pretty to look at, but it is safer to watch them from inside your warm house!

Glossary

cold front   The edge of a cold air mass.

dangerous   Able to cause harm.

drift   A large pile of snow blown by the wind.

freeze   To be turned from a liquid to a solid by the cold, such as when water turns to ice.

frostbite   Harm to uncovered skin caused by very cold weather.

snowstorm   A storm with a lot of snow.

water vapor   Tiny drops of water in the air.

whiteout   When snow is blown around by wind, making it hard to see.

windchill   The effect of cold air and high wind speed that makes weather seem colder than it is.

Index

C
cold front, 10

D
drifts, 5

F
frostbite, 13

G
Great Plains, 6

I
ice, 9

N
northern states, 6

S
snow, 5, 9, 10
snowflakes, 9
snowstorm, 5

W
water vapor, 9
whiteout(s), 5, 6
windchill, 13
winds, 5, 9, 10, 13